BUZZ ALDRIN

REACHING FOR THE MOON

PAINTINGS BY
WENDELL MINOR

Rutland Free Library
10 Court Street
Rutland, VT 05701-4058

COLLINS

AN IMPRINT OF HARPERCOLLINSPUBLISHERS

Collins is an imprint of HarperCollins Publishers.

For more information about the *Apollo 11* Moon landing please visit www.nasa.gov or The Johnson Space Center at www.jsc.nasa.gov, and for more information about the illustrations in this book please visit www.minorart.com.

Wendell Minor wishes to acknowledge NASA, the Johnson Space Center, and the Buzz Aldrin family for providing reference material for this book.

Reaching for the Moon   Text copyright © 2005 by Buzz Aldrin   Illustrations copyright © 2005 by Wendell Minor
Manufactured in China. All rights reserved. For information address HarperCollins Children's Books, a division of
HarperCollins Publishers, 195 Broadway, New York, NY 10007.   www.harpercollinschildrens.com

Library of Congress Cataloging-in-Publication Data   Aldrin, Buzz.   Reaching for the moon / Buzz Aldrin ; paintings
by Wendell Minor.— 1st ed.   p. cm.   ISBN 978-0-06-055445-3 (trade bdg.) — ISBN 978-0-06-055446-0 (lib. bdg.)
— ISBN 978-0-06-055447-7 (pbk.)   1. Aldrin, Buzz—Juvenile literature. 2. Astronauts—United States—Biography—
Juvenile literature. 3. Space flight to the moon—Juvenile literature. 4. Project Apollo (U.S.)—Juvenile literature.
I. Minor, Wendell, ill. II. Title.   TL789.85.A4A3 2005   2004006247   629.45'0092—dc22

Typography by Wendell Minor and Al Cetta   ❖   First Edition
16 SCP 20 19 18 17 16 15

First came the original astronaut explorers,
those of Mercury, Gemini, and Apollo.
Then came the next generation,
flying shuttle missions to the space station.
Now is the time to venture outward and
   see new wonders. . . .
Now is the time for the youth of today,
the third generation of future space explorers.
                              —*Buzz Aldrin*

In memory of Bob Schulman—friend, artist,
and former director of the NASA Art Program.
                              — *Wendell Minor*

The name my parents gave me was Edwin Eugene, but the name my sister gave me was the one that would stay with me all my life. Since I was the only son, everyone in my family called me Brother. But my sister Fay Ann, a year older than I was, could only manage to say "Buzzer." Later it got shortened to "Buzz," and no one ever called me anything else.

On summer nights the Moon hung low in the sky, so close to our house that I thought I could reach out and touch the soft white light. I never imagined that one day I would walk on its surface. But maybe it was meant to be. You see, before she was married, my mother's last name was Moon.

My father's job with Standard Oil took him all over the country, and he flew his own plane from coast to coast. During World War II he served in the Army Air Corps and came home for visits, looking tall and important in his colonel's uniform.

When I was two years old, my father took me flying for the first time, in a small, shiny white plane painted to look like an eagle. I was a little frightened as the plane shuddered into flight. But mostly I was thrilled. I loved the speed, the sense of soaring high above the Earth, supported only by the air passing around the metal wings.

One day I would fly in a different machine called the *Eagle*—but that would be many years in the future and a very different kind of adventure.

Usually there was plenty to hold my attention right here on Earth. My family spent many summers at Culver Lake in the Appalachian Mountains, and one summer, when I was about six or seven, I began collecting rocks. There was treasure everywhere I looked. Those rocks were precious, they were beautiful, and—most importantly—they were *mine*.

One morning I gathered up the best of my rocks, put them in a bucket, and carried them down to the dock to show my friend. He wanted a rock. I didn't want to give it to him. He pushed me, bucket and all, off the dock.

I wouldn't let go of my rocks, even though the weight of them pulled me down. The light at the surface slowly drifted away. When my friend's father pulled me out, I still had my arms wrapped around the bucket.

I knew that if something was important to you, you had to hold on.

Determination, strength, independence—those were the qualities I worshipped in my favorite movie hero, the Lone Ranger. I went to the movies every Saturday, and sometimes I even snuck in through the fire escape when I didn't have the money to buy a ticket. I felt just like the Lone Ranger the day I set off to ride my bike across the George Washington Bridge to New York City. Ten years old, I pedaled twenty miles down unfamiliar roads and busy streets, past neighbors and strangers, out into the unknown. Just like the Lone Ranger, I didn't need help from anyone. It took me all day, but I found the way and did it myself.

Almost every day I played some kind of sport, from swimming to high school track to pick-up games of football in the park across the street. The older boys let me play because although I was small, I was tough.

No matter what the sport, I played every game hard, because I wanted to win. I loved being part of a team, working together to fight for victory. But it was even better to compete on my own, like when I flew over the bar in pole-vaulting. Then it was just me trying, with everything I had, to be the best. Whether I won or lost was up to me.

When I finished high school, my father wanted me to go to the naval academy, but I chose West Point instead. I wasn't interested in the Navy; I wanted to be in the Air Force. And I thought West Point would help me get there.

That first summer at West Point was the toughest challenge I had faced. We had to run everywhere; no walking was allowed. We couldn't speak during meals. Every order from an upperclassman or a teacher had to be obeyed at once.

I followed every order. I studied every night. By the end of the year I was first in my class. By the end of four years I had the grades to do whatever I wanted—and what I wanted more than anything was to fly!

After West Point I joined the Air Force, at last, and learned to fly fighter jets, fast and quick in the sky. I loved the feeling of breaking free from gravity. I loved going as fast as a human being could go.

When I finished my training, I flew sixty-six combat missions in the Korean War.

After the war I was stationed in Germany, learning to pilot planes that flew faster than the speed of sound. But there were men flying faster than that—America's first seven astronauts, the men in the Mercury program. Their goal was to be the first Americans to orbit the earth.

The astronauts seemed like supermen to me. I couldn't imagine myself exploring outer space. But that changed when my friend Ed White from West Point told me his plan to apply to the space program. That was when I realized that the Mercury astronauts were pilots just like Ed—and just like me. I already flew the fastest planes on Earth. But Mercury was a brand-new adventure. It was America's first step into space. And I wanted to be a part of it.

I was already a good pilot. But the Air Force had many good pilots. I needed to find something I could do better than anyone else, something that would make me an astronaut.

I went back to a university, to the same school my father had gone to, and studied aeronautics and astronautics. I specialized in something called rendezvous, learning how to bring two different objects together in space.

Computers could do most of the work for rendezvous, but I believed that pilots needed to understand it themselves, in case something went wrong. A computer can calculate numbers faster than the human brain; but people bring creativity and common sense to a problem, something a computer cannot do.

I dedicated my final paper to the American astronauts: "Oh, that I were one of them."

The first time I applied to the astronaut program, I wasn't accepted. But I didn't give up. When I applied a second time, I got in. I tried to appear as if I'd always known I'd make it, but inside I was bursting with excitement. I was already a pilot and a scientist: now I was an astronaut as well.

Along with the other men in the space program, I studied computers and instruments, what went right and what went wrong on each previous spaceflight, and how to survive in the wilderness if my spacecraft crashed returning to Earth. We also had to learn to move in the weightlessness of space. The others trained with a system of ropes and pulleys, but I thought training underwater would work much better. I spent hours in the pool tethered to an air line. The simplest movements—turning a handle, tightening a screw—had to be practiced over and over again.

My first spaceflight was on board *Gemini 12*. My mission, along with my fellow astronaut Jim Lovell, was to orbit the Earth and to practice rendezvous techniques with another vehicle in space.

Once the spacecraft was in orbit, I put on my space suit, opened the hatch, and drifted out into space. Only a thin cord connected me to *Gemini* as we circled the Earth at 17,500 miles per hour, five miles every second. It took us less than two hours to go all the way around the world.

But the speed didn't seem real to me. I felt as if I were gently floating while the Earth spun beneath me. I could see the great curve of my home planet: the brown mass of Africa, night falling over the Indian Ocean, a shower of green meteors tumbling into the Australian desert.

After *Gemini 12*, there was a new mission — Apollo. The goal of Apollo was to put humans on the Moon.

Many people thought it couldn't be done. They thought that the powerful rockets needed to go that far could never be built. They thought that computers could never do all the calculations. They thought that, even if we did reach the Moon, we would never be able to take off again to come home. But, one by one, all the challenges were met.

Neil Armstrong, Mike Collins, and I were next in line for a spaceflight, so we were chosen as the team for *Apollo 11* — the flight that would land on the Moon.

Three years after my Gemini mission, I stood beside *Apollo 11*'s Saturn V rocket. It was sunrise on July 16, 1969. Neil and Mike were already in their places on board. For a few moments I was alone.

All my life I had struggled to learn, to compete, to succeed, so that I could be what I was in that one moment: an astronaut on a mission to the Moon. I felt nothing but calm confidence. I was sure we would make it there and back.

It was time for me to board.

Neil, Mike, and I lay side by side on three couches, tightly strapped in. Beneath us I heard a rumble, like a faraway train. But as we lifted off, the movement felt so gentle that if I had not been looking at the instruments, I would never have known we were on our way.

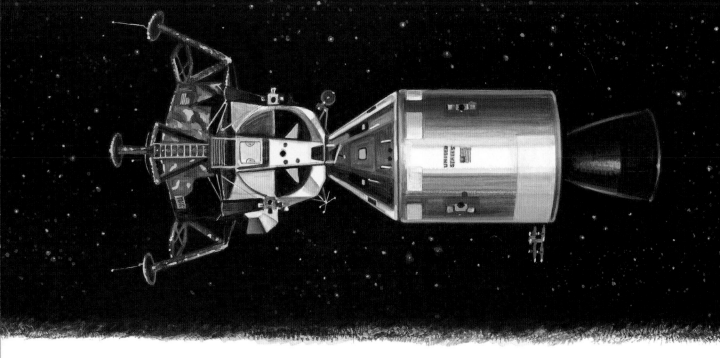

Outside the window of the *Apollo 11*, the Earth grew smaller and smaller. At last we were so far away that I could hold up my thumb and block the bright disk from my sight.

After five hours we could take off our space suits and helmets and move around the cabin. We ate chicken salad and applesauce for dinner, with shrimp cocktail, my favorite of our freeze-dried choices. Then it was time to rest. Wrapped in sleeping bags, we floated above the couches, comfortably weightless. For this time *Apollo 11* was our home, a tiny bubble of air and warmth speeding through the icy cold of space.

Four days after launch, and after traveling 240,000 miles, we were in orbit around the Moon. *Apollo* separated into two parts: *Columbia*, where Mike would wait in orbit, and the *Eagle*, the lander. The *Eagle* was powerful enough to take Neil and me down to the Moon's surface and back up to *Columbia*. But its walls were so thin, I could have punched a pencil through them if I had tried.

The computer had chosen a spot for
the *Eagle* to land. But through the window we could see that
it was too rocky. We couldn't rely on the computer to land the
Eagle safely. We would have to do it ourselves.

Neil took control. I called out to let him know how far we
were from the ground. Two hundred feet. One hundred.
Forty. By the time the *Eagle* landed, we had used up almost all
our fuel with only twenty seconds left to spare.

But we had made it. We were safely on the surface of the
Moon. I grinned at Neil. There was no need to say anything.
We had work to do.

Flight and spaceflight had always meant motion to me. But now the *Eagle* stood perfectly still.

Neil and I put on our space suits. Neil climbed out first and descended *Eagle*'s ladder to the Moon's surface. Everyone listening back on Earth heard Neil's first words: "That's one small step for . . . man, one giant leap for mankind."

I climbed down the ladder and joined Neil. There was no color on the Moon. A flat landscape of rocks and craters stretched in all directions. Everything was gray or white. The shadows and the sky above were as black as the blackest velvet I had ever seen. I exclaimed: "Magnificent desolation."

I could see Earth, our home, in the sky overhead—blue water, white clouds, and brown land. I could see the continents, and I knew that they were younger than the Moon dust in which Neil and I were now leaving our footprints.

I took out the American flag from the compartment where it was stored.

Neil and I could force the pole only a few inches into the Moon's soil. I knew that more than half a billion people back on Earth were watching on television, and I worried that the flag would sag or tip. But when we took our hands away, it stood straight. I snapped off a crisp salute, just as I was taught at West Point.

We moved quickly on to other tasks. I became a rock collector again, gathering samples for study back on Earth.

Still, I remember that brief moment perfectly, so many years later. I remember the pride I felt and how I imagined the pride of every American on Earth.

Neil and I set up a plaque that would remain on the surface of the Moon with the simple words:

HERE MEN FROM THE PLANET EARTH

FIRST SET FOOT UPON THE MOON

JULY 1969, A.D.

WE CAME IN PEACE FOR ALL MANKIND

In 1961 President John F. Kennedy made a speech challenging Americans to land a person on the Moon by 1970. By 1969 we had achieved that goal. It took engineering genius and hard work. It took teamwork and individual skill. It took courage and sacrifice. Apollo was a success. Humans walked on the surface of another world.

Neil and I were only the first. In all, twelve astronauts have visited the Moon. However, twenty-two men and women from around the world have died exploring space. One of them was my good friend Ed White, who first gave me the idea of becoming an astronaut.

Since the Moon landing, I have worked to promote our future in space. The early NASA programs—Mercury, Gemini, and Apollo—were just a beginning. Someday humans will travel farther than the Moon. I believe we will go to the other planets in our solar system, perhaps live permanently on the Moon or on Mars. One day you may buy a ticket on a spaceship as easily as you buy an airplane ticket today.

Perhaps some of these ideas seem impossible. But many people thought the same about our mission to the Moon. Having a goal, even one that seems beyond our reach, can inspire us to achieve something magnificent.

Not everyone can explore space. But we all have our own moons to reach for. If you set your sights high, you may accomplish more than you ever dreamed was possible. Just as I did.

Buzz Aldrin

Buzz Aldrin and a Century of Flight and Space Exploration

1903 Wilbur and Orville Wright achieve the first manned, powered flight on Kill
Devil Hill near Kitty Hawk, North Carolina.

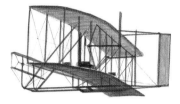

1909 Louis Blériot is the first person to fly across the English Channel.

1926 Robert H. Goddard launches the first liquid-fueled rocket, the forerunner of all
the rockets used in the space program today.

1927 Charles Lindbergh is the first to fly solo across the Atlantic Ocean.

1930 Edwin Eugene "Buzz" Aldrin Jr. is born in Montclair, New Jersey, on
January 20.

1932 Amelia Earhart is the first woman to fly solo across the Atlantic Ocean.

1933 Wiley Post is the first to fly solo around the world.

1947 Chuck Yeager is the first to fly faster than the speed of sound.

1951 Buzz Aldrin graduates from West Point and joins the Air Force.

1952–53 Buzz Aldrin flies sixty-six combat missions in an F-86 Sabre jet in the Korean War.

1955 Buzz Aldrin is stationed in Bitburg, Germany, and flies the F-100 jet faster than
the speed of sound.

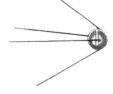

1957 The Soviet Union launches *Sputnik*, the first man-made satellite to orbit Earth.

1961 Yuri A. Gagarin, in the *Vostok 1*, is the first human to orbit Earth.

1961   Mercury astronaut Alan B. Shepard Jr., in the *Freedom 7*, is the first American in space.

1962   Mercury astronaut John H. Glenn, in the *Friendship 7*, is the first American to orbit Earth.

1963   Buzz Aldrin graduates from the Massachusetts Institute of Technology with a doctoral degree in astronautics and is accepted into the NASA astronaut program.

1965   The U.S. launches *Gemini 4*. Ed White performs the first American space walk, twenty-three minutes long.

1966   The U.S. launches *Gemini 12*. Buzz performs three separate space walks, for a total of five hours and thirty minutes in space.

1967   Virgil "Gus" Grissom, Ed White, and Roger Chaffee are killed in an explosion aboard the *Apollo 1* during a preflight test.

1969   The U.S. launches *Apollo 11*. Neil Armstrong and Buzz Aldrin land on the Moon.

1981   The U.S. launches the space shuttle *Columbia*.

1986   The space shuttle *Challenger* is destroyed, killing all seven crew members, including the first civilian in space, teacher Christa McAuliffe.

1990   The Hubble Space Telescope is launched.

1996   Buzz Aldrin founds Starcraft Boosters, Inc., to design technology for spaceflight.

1997   The Mars Pathfinder mission lands the *Sojourner* rover on Mars.

1998   Construction of the International Space Station begins.

1998   Buzz Aldrin establishes the ShareSpace Foundation, working to make spaceflight available to everyone.

2003   The space shuttle *Columbia* is destroyed while returning to Earth, killing all seven crew members.

2003   China launches the *Shenzhou 5*. Yang Liwei orbits the Earth.

2004   The thirty-fifth anniversary of *Apollo 11*'s Moon landing on July 20, 1969.